I'm A Pretty Little Black Girl!

Written by
Betty K. Bynum

Illustrated by
Claire Armstrong Parod

For my Mama,

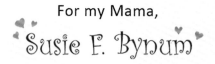
Susie F. Bynum

who was prettier than she ever realized.

And for Joshua and Warren,
I love you both with all my heart.

Text © 2013 Betty K. Bynum
Illustrations © 2013 DreamTitle Publishing/Workhouse Road Productions
The I'm A Girl Collection™
The I'm A Girl Collection © 2013
www.theimagirlcollection.com

Author/Art Director/Editor: Betty K. Bynum
Illustrator/Design/Type and Page Layouts: Claire Armstrong Parod
Graphic Designer: Brian Boehm
Creative Consultant: Lawrence Christmas
Special thanks to Joel Parod

ISBN Hardback: 978-0-615-7855-1-6
ISBN ebook: 978-0-615-7424-9-6
LCCN: 2013939365

First Edition
Printed in China
14 13 12 11 10 09 1 2 3 4 5 6 7 8 9 10

I look in the mirror,
and on some days,

My hair is just-a-going
every which-a-ways!

And when I see myself
in the mirror,

I twirl,

And I yell,

"I'm a Pretty Little Black Girl!"

I start to **dance** 'cause nobody's looking,

I dance like
cra-aa-AAA-ZY!

The only thing that stops me is the smell of something cooking!

I eat...
grab my
school books...

and I start right out the door.

BUT!........ Before I leave, I STOP...
to see myself
from head to floor...

I LAUGH
and SPIN
AGAIN

with a great,
big, dizzy, TWIRL,

And say, "YES! ...I'm a Pretty Little Black Girl!"

I walk with friends
to school,

Our noisy steps
are "clucks" and "clatter".

Our other friends
                are waiting there,

as we all chirp
and chatter!

At our secret meeting place...

(Shhh... the flowers by the wall),

I glance at each girl's happy face,

I glance
at them all:

My friend Kia...

...is tall and tan,

My friend Keisha is the color of pecan;

My best friend Charlotte...

...is like milk in coffee.

Dina-Rosemarie
is the color
of toffee.

Imani
in my class
is like
sweet dark
chocolate cream,

Her magical smile glows
like she was kissed
by moonbeams!

Active Anna's hair
is red with twists
and crinkly-spun,

She is the
just-about-almost color
of sprinkling cinnamon.

When Ruby sings
her head moves
so her braids
just sway
and swag,

Her dark eyes shine
like marbles
in a brown
paper bag!

Tracy is the color
of a buttercup daisy,

Is it her
honey-colored hair
that drives bees
crazy?

But all of our colors

blended into one,

Makes

us

Pretty

Black

girls

and we

have our fun!

We all

join hands

like

a

chain

no one

can break,

We might skip and laugh, play jack rocks,

Jump rope or roller skate. If one of us falls, the other one picks her up.

If one of us cries,

the other uses her dress hem......

......to dry the tears up.

We come in all shapes and sizes-
skinny, short or round,
And like a
special rainbow
we're all different
shades of brown.

We say
"PLEASE"
and
"THANK YOU"
That's how we

spread Love around!

I think of what "Pretty" is, and this is what I find:
"Pretty" also means "to show GOOD MANNERS"
all the time!

When we are
still and
quiet,
I just
THINK
of all of us

And hope that we
will always be
GOOD FRIENDS
that never roll their eyes
or hate, or fight or fuss:

'Cause tan or pecan,

Or buttercup daisy,

or sweet dark chocolate cream,

Or anything in between......

We're gonna grow up to show the world

some BRILLIANCE

it ain't never seen!

See you all tomorrow!
BYE!

At the end of my day
right before
I go to bed,

All my friends' smiling faces start to flash inside my head.

My legs then start to fidget,

like they're too happy to sleep,

So I jump up out of bed,

'cause now

the happy's in my feet!

My Mom yells, "Mia! Sweetheart... it's time to go to sleep!"

BUT!..... I DANCE
and TWIRL

again

as if all

my friends

were there;

My going every which-a-ways,

fluffy,

curly,

bouncy,

twisty,

springy,

HAPPY HAIR!

Then I stop a while -
take a breath and slow my pace,
I take a LONG, LONG
look at my nutmeg-colored face.

For a moment then,
I stare - I think - and make a frown,
My clothes all-crazy 'round my waist,
my socks all-falling down;

THEN!...........

I LAUGH

OUT LOUD

at myself!

Stretch out

my arms

and make a

BIGGER

TWIRL!!!

Spinning

FASTER....!!!

Yelling LOUDER!!!....

"I'M A
PRETTY
LITTLE BLACK GIRL!!!"